PB

The Best Blanket

by Sarah Nash
illustrated by Pamela Venus

Tamarind Ltd

"Your blanket's so smelly, Donna," said Mum.
"Shall we wash it?"

"Your blanket's worn out," said Dad.
"Shall we get a new one?"

"NO!" shouted Donna.
"I need my blanket.
I will keep it forever!"

"*It's my scarf on cold days...*"

"...my bag on busy days..."

"...my island on lonely days..."

"...my tent on camping days..."

when I'm scared."

"I love
my blanket.
It's the BEST
blanket
in the world!"

Look out for other Tamarind titles:

Picture books

A Safe Place

I Don't Eat Toothpaste Anymore!

Giant Hiccups

Dave and the Tooth Fairy

ABC I Can Be

Caribbean Animals

Are We There Yet?

Boots for a Bridesmaid

Board books

Baby Noises

Baby Plays

Baby Goes

Baby Finds

Let's Have Fun

Let's Go to Playgroup

Let's Go to Bed

Let's Feed the Ducks

Published by Tamarind Ltd, 2005
PO Box 52
Northwood
Middx HA6 1UN
UK

Text © Sarah Nash
Illustrations © Pamela Venus
Edited by Simona Sideri
Cover design by Sarah Hodder

ISBN 1 870516 63 X

Printed in China